SOME PEOPLE
BY DANNY HOCH

Copyright © 1993, 1998 Danny Hoch. All rights reserved.
Original front cover design © 1994 Paula Scher/Pentagram. Used by permission.
Front and back cover photos: Paula Court. Used by permission.
Cover and photo montage: Kiku & Skwerm.
Editorial/production consulting: Greg Gattuso.

Some People is published by Caseroc Productions
c/o Washington Square Arts, 12 East 10th Street, New York, NY 10003.

Except for brief passages quoted in newspaper, magazine, radio or television reviews, no part of this book may be reproduced in any form by any means, electronic or mechanical, including photocopying or recording, or by an information storage and retrieval system, without permission in writing from the publisher.

CAUTION: Professionals and amateurs are hereby warned that this material, the play *Some People* and the monologues from *Some People* are subject to a royalty. The play and monologues are fully protected under the Copyright Laws of the United States of America and all other countries of the Berne and Universal Copyright Conventions, International Copyright Union (including the Dominion of Canada and the rest of the British Commonwealth). All rights including, but not limited to, professional, amateur, recording, motion picture, recitation, lecturing, public reading, radio and television broadcasting, and the rights of translation into foreign languages are expressly reserved. Although theatre students are encouraged to use this material in their studies, particular emphasis is placed on the question of readings and all uses of this play by educational institutions, permission for which must be secured by author's agents: Peter Hagan, Gersh Agency, 130 West 42nd Street, New York, NY 10036 (212) 997-1818. Kathleen Russo, Washington Square Arts, 12 East 10th Street, New York, NY 10003 (212) 253-0333.

All characters and personas printed in this book are fictitious. Any similarity to actual persons, living or dead, is purely coincidental and unintentional.

Library Of Congress Cataloging-in-Publication Data
Some People/by Danny Hoch
ISBN No. 0-9663506-0-X
Library of Congress Catalog Card Number: 98-84754
1.American Drama-20th Century. 2. Monologues.
3. Monodramas. 4. Performance Art. 5. Urban Studies. I. Title.
Hoch, Danny

First edition March 1998

Manufactured in the United States of America

To purchase additional copies of this book, or for general information, contact:
Performance Associates (212) 620-4866 or Washington Square Arts (212) 253-0333

BY DANNY HOCH

Published by Caseroc Productions
c/o Washington Square Arts,
12 East 10th Street, New York, NY 10003.

Copyright © 1993, 1998 Danny Hoch. All rights reserved.

First Edition March 1998

ACKNOWLEDGMENTS

There are many people to thank, without whom this work could not have been possible. My director, Jo Bonney, who made me write down the oral language spewing from my mouthpiece. JT Rogers, Gus Reyes and the Next Stage Company who were there with me in a freezing gas station hanging lights and sticking posters all over Avenue B, Greg Freelon, David Ellis, Mark Russell, P.S. 122, Dominick Balletta, The Jerome Foundation, Shelby Jiggetts-Tivony, Morgan Jenness, George Wolfe, The Joseph Papp Public Theater, The Solo Mio Festival in San Francisco, Baltimore Theatre Project, William McLaughlin, David Campbell, Jon Rubin, Bridgette Potter, Robert Small, John Fortenberry, Greg Gattuso, Kiku Yamaguchi, Paula Court, Dona Ann McAdams, Paula Scher, Nchito, Yaurelita, Brooklyn-Queens Nation, Leah Nelson, Greg Hubbard, NYU's Creative Arts Team. And most importantly, my audience, my friends and family who keep coming to the shows. Without you, there is no performance.

CONTENTS

Introduction	xi
Caribbean Tiger (plus callers)	1
Madman	9
Kazmierczack	13
Floe	15
Bill	21
Blanca	29
Al Capón	35
Doris	37
Flex	43
César	49
Roughneck Chicken (epilogue)	55

For My Mother

. . . who taught me how to really listen

INTRODUCTION

Peace yo! Welcome to my book. I'm a third-generation New Yorker, lucky enough to grow up during the birth of Hip-Hop culture in a towering brick-and-asphalt outer-borough neighborhood, where there was no racial majority or minority. I trained as an actor, to play everything from Moliere to Tennessee Williams to Sam Shepard to Samuel Beckett to Shakespeare, even Neil Simon. It was invaluable, and probably saved my life from some of my teenage ill-street escapades.

There was one problem. Although my teachers were wonderful, I was being trained to drop the languages I grew up with. In order to be a "successful" actor, I was supposed to forget all of the rich language that was my whole cultural foundation. I was destined to be in a Broadway or off-Broadway show, movie or TV show that had nothing to do with the people or stories from my community, or even to do with my generation. Tom Stoppard and Harold Pinter don't write about Grandmaster Flash or Disco Bar-Mitzvahs or Mofongo. *Showboat* and *Sideshow* ain't don't got nothin' to do with my life. To put it Brooklyn-style, I had mad beef with this situation.

Theatre is *about* language. Oral, physical and spiritual language, and that's it. If I can't relate to the universality of the character's language; if I'm excluded by the abstraction of the art taking place; if I live in Brooklyn and all I get to see is *Arcadia, Home Improvement, The English Patient* and *The Martin Lawrence Show,* then what's the point? There is no pathos, no catharsis whatsoever in the intellectual bullshit that calls itself art and entertainment. We sit there thinking about the holes in our socks. Or maybe we laugh or cry. But all we're permitted to do is laugh and cry at the characters, not at ourselves. We sit passively entertained, instead of actively engaged.

I wanted no part of this theatre. It defies the theatre's intentions. Theatre is for the people. Not just *some* people. Somewhere around when I was eighteen, I decided to make my own theatre. All of the stories, voices and characters that *I* felt were important, I put on stage. I "wrote" it all orally in front of audiences. The characters were not confined to a page. They were alive, allowed to breathe, to go wherever they wanted. I called it structured improvisation. Eventually, I would keep the good stuff and get rid of the bad stuff, and boom—I had a show. It was called *Pot Melting*, and the few thousand people who saw it back in the early 1990s will remember that it changed a bit from show to show, because I never really wrote down any of the dozen characters that I created. It was oral theatre, the ancient way, but with modern themes and today's language.

I had the same approach to *Some People*. Although this time, I worked with a director, Jo Bonney. I needed someone with an outside eye. I was reluctant to do this for many reasons.

First off, usually what directors do is take a script, digest it, interpret it, and stage it according to their personal, inspired "artistic vision." How do you collaborate when it's *your* vision?

How do you direct oral language? How do you help shape voices that already have their own distinct shapes? How do you *direct* something that is improvised?

I found out very quickly, it didn't matter that my director couldn't tell the difference between Jamaican and Trinidadian Patois. What was important was that she understood how the social function of theatre operates, that really we are blue-collar workers that happen to manufacture popular, provocative, storyline educational entertainment. She also understood the relationship between the solo actor and the audience. A relationship that is often looked at, not as theater, but as stand-up comedy (an entirely different dynamic). What theater director knows how to stage a play with a cast of one?

The first thing she did was make me actually write down what happened orally on stage and look at it. I was horrified. I always felt (and still feel) that sitting and writing is more of an intellectual, mathematical way of creating, as opposed to creating in front of an audience, which is purely visceral. Visceral is what theatre is supposed to be!

But okay, I submit. There's something to be said for writing things down. For the first time, I actually saw what I was saying—dramaturgically. This helped me shape a better "structure" to work from while I was on stage. Basically, it refined the visceral fragmented storytelling riffs into clarified visceral stories that sounded like riffs.

Solo theatre is something very ancient in nature. It pre-dates the Romans and the Greeks and can be found in the indigenous theatres of Africa, Asia and the Americas (before European

SOME PEOPLE

colonialism). When the French were colonizing Africa, they used the word *griot* to describe the various solo performers they encountered. People who used drama, comedy, pantomime, storytelling, dance, music, possession and masks to create community performance. They reflected, celebrated, reconstructed and questioned their lives. In other words, pure unfiltered theatre. They were shamans, teachers, preachers, actors and social critics—all in one.

In the United States, because of our young sense of cultural history, we are not terribly familiar with solo theatre. We are, however, accustomed to stand-up comedians, talk-show hosts, mimes, magicians, politicians, rabbis and priests. Those are the solo performers we are accustomed to. Well, I wanted to be an urban *griot* for the communities of urban NorthAmerica.

I don't tape-record or interview people to then play them on stage. A few people think I am some anthropological/theatrical case-study guy. This is my world! These are my inner monologues, layered composites of stories and voices from me, my family, my neighborhood, my people. I think all the hoopla about my work comes from people not being accustomed to seeing traditionally *peripheral* characters in a center-stage setting. Well, these characters are center-stage in *my* world.

Contrary to what many purveyors of theatre would have us think, NorthAmerica isn't just people who live near strip malls in two-story houses somewhere in the suburbs. This nation is teeming with communities where rich people and middle class White people are *not* at the center; yet we see who is deemed deserving of our stage time.

I often wonder if my skin were darker, or if I couldn't flip my linguistics during meetings to sound *"businesslike and un-threatening"* (I swear somebody said that to me), if I would have had the success I've had with *Some People*. Was I a "safe in" to the *"disenfranchised voices of America"* for the rich and middle class? Maybe. This country is some wild shit.

A lot of Hollywood people saw *Some People*, and I was offered several opportunities to write and act in television and film. Seeing them happen was another story. I'm actually not surprised at the resistance I've come up against in the entertainment/media/propaganda industry, when trying to get three-dimensional poor characters and non-Eurocentric characters into mainstream storylines. I just never imagined that producers and publishers and studio executives would blatantly say things like, *"People don't want to watch Puertoricans . . ."* or *"America is mostly White people. You don't want to dis-interest them . . ."* or *"It's funnier with the Black accent."* (What is a Black accent?) or *"You can't have a piece entirely in Spanish—who's gonna get it?"* Wow, right? Shit is real out there.

One last thing—although this is a book of monologues, this is a play. It is a book of monologues which *is* a play. Although I wrote *Some People* down (like my director told me to), the characters have evolved over the course of many performances. Even after *Some People* opened at P.S. 122, the Public Theater and throughout touring it, it changed. This edition is based on the last round of shows I did in 1996, and contains the full, uncut monologues that appeared in the 1995 HBO special, as well as three other pieces from the original live show that didn't make it to HBO—*Madman*, *Al Capón* and *Flex*.

SOME PEOPLE

If the reader is interested in other contemporary solo theatre, I would highly recommend checking out the works of Rhodessa Jones, Dael Orlandersmith, Peggy Pettitt and Roger Guenveur Smith. They will blow your mind, and your mind needs to get blown if you live in *this* country.

Peace Out . . .

Danny Hoch
Brooklyn, New York
January 1998

SOME PEOPLE
BY DANNY HOCH

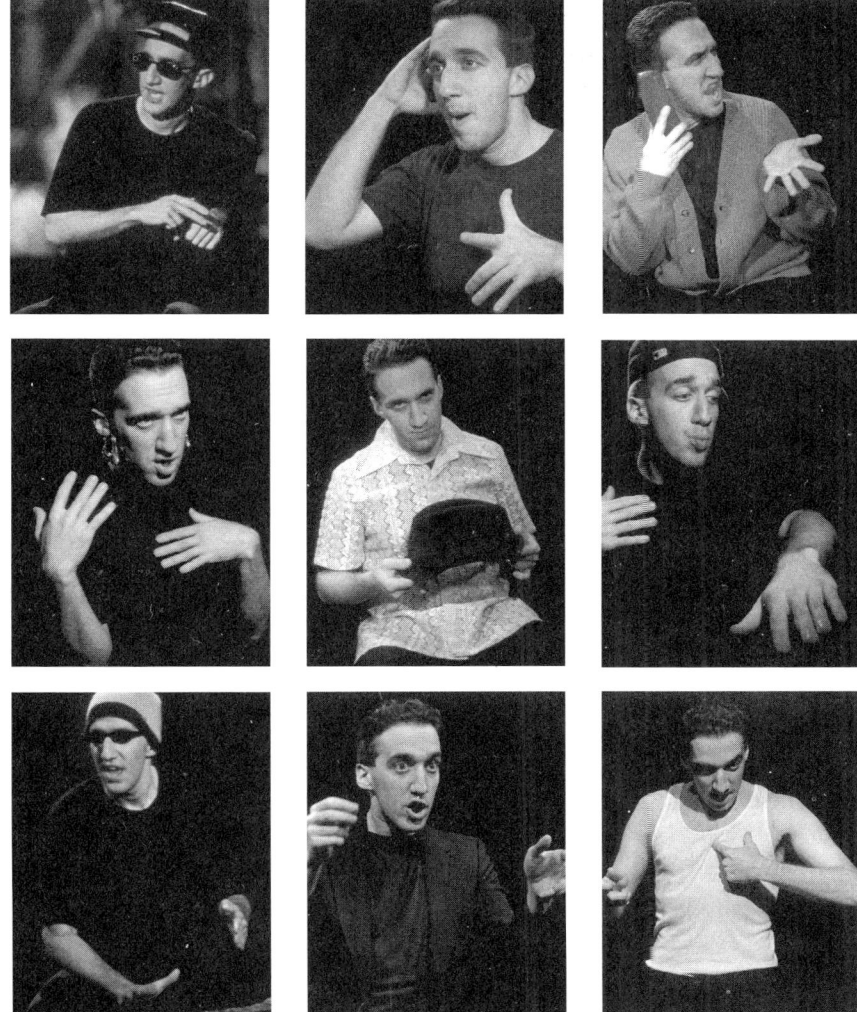

The only set to this show is a black wooden cube about knee-high, a black stool and a black chair. These three are moved around in different configurations for each character.

A clothesline hangs upstage from which the minimal costume pieces hang by clothespins.

An open cardboard box for used costumes sits under the clothesline. The costumes are merely accessories to a constant black jeans, T-shirt and shoes. A hat, sweater, blazer or headphones are grabbed from the clothesline and tossed on quickly for each character change.

CARIBBEAN TIGER

[*The scene is a dimly lit radio studio at around one in the morning. The callers, Daddy Sluggy, Clyde and Sheila are pre-recorded.*]

Mmm! Yes ladies and gentlemen of the Big Apple this is Vaughn Morris your host. Better known to all my fans out there as the Caribbean Tiger! Some people say, what's a tiger doin in the Caribbean, people well I tell you livin up ya inna New York City is like a jungle sometimes and anything can happen, just like a Tiger walkin by upon your radio waves.

Who is listenin to me? Who is stayin up with me this early morning, Friday morning, a few minutes after one o'clock people I'd like to know. Call me call me call me. The phone number is 718-282-2828, that's 718-282-2828. The temperature outside right now the weatherman says! About twenty-seven degrees ice cold people. I tellin ya, ya better buncle up and stay warm it's cold outside but never if you're riding with me here upon the radio waves Caribbean Tiger Style! Like the man says, you're riding with the Tiger you know it gotta be Hot! Vaughn Morris Comes Rough Every Time. Vaughn Morris Is A First Class Tiger.

Mmm, yes people I'm comin mixin up your Reggae, Rockers, Soca and Calypso, oldies but goodies. This hour strictly Soca music! We goin see if you can wind your waist one time. I am lookin at my telephone switchboard now, my phone lines is blinkin people! Wild fire inna studio! Worries and Trouble! I'm going to the phones right now . . . Hello good morning you're on the air . . .

DADDY SLUGGY: Ere dat boss. Wha'appnin Mister Morris?

Who am I talkin with this morning?

DADDY SLUGGY: Disya Daddy Sluggy, seen.

Daddy Sluggy! Ok Daddy Sluggy where you callin from?

DADDY SLUGGY: Me inna Brooklyn, yeh.

Ok Daddy Sluggy from Brooklyn, you ever call before?

DADDY SLUGGY: Na boss. Aeda check you show fe years, but si is a first time me a pick up de phone an call you pon radio station, seen.

Alright Daddy Sluggy you want to send some greetings out there?

DADDY SLUGGY: Yeah boss. Ya know first I wan say big up to Pudgy, Mikey, Tinga and Gary over there in East Flatbush Love Productions. Special request to Big Timer crew, Sleepy, and all Jamaican people dem, beca ya know seh Jamaica people dem ago run tings inna New York City.

Ok respect to you brother.

DADDY SLUGGY: Yeah and greetins comin from Daddy Sluggy.

Ok Daddy Sluggy you have a good night now. You're riding with the most dangerous DJ on the radio, I am the Caribbean Tiger. Raaar! Watchout Baby! Hello good morning you're on the air . . .

CLYDE: Eh . . .

Hello good morning.

CLYDE: Yes.

Yes hello.

CLYDE: Yes. . . . Hello?

Yes good morning sir.

CLYDE: Am I on de radio?

Yes you on the radio, would you like to send some greetings out there?

CLYDE: Oh. Yeah. I want to say hello to Roberta, who just arrive yesterday from Port of Spain.

And this is comin from?

CLYDE: Excuse me?

Wha is you name sir?

CLYDE: Oh. Clyde.

Ok Clyde, where are you callin me from Clyde?

CLYDE: . . . Yeah.

Yeah, where are you callin me from?

CLYDE: Huh?

Where are you? Where are you Clyde?

CLYDE: Brooklyn.

Ok Clyde from Brooklyn thanks for callin in alright?

CLYDE: Ok Bye bye.

Ok yes people, the Caribbean Tiger is in the house tonight! Good mornin you're on the air.

SHEILA: Good morning Caribbean Tiger.

Whoa ho ho! The Caribbean Tiger is most definitely in the place tonight! Who is this?

SHEILA: This is Sheila. How are you Mister Morris?

Fine sweetheart, how are you?

SHEILA: Is this a tape? Or am I really on the radio?

Fine sweetheart, how are you?

SHEILA: No, seriously is this real?

Hello, good morning?

SHEILA: Is this you Mr. Morris?

Fine sweetheart, how are you?

SHEILA: Stop it, that's no fair.

Ha! Ha! Ha! I'm just playin with you Sheila. You really tink I'm a tape? Lemme tell you somethin Sheila I am live no jive, never contrive, and I play all you disco forty-five. Raar! Where are you callin me from Sheila?

SHEILA: Brooklyn.

Sheila from Brooklyn, are you married?

SHEILA: No.

Do you have a boyfriend?

SHEILA: Yes.

Do you think your boyfriend would mind if I ask you on a date? Because you sound like the prettiest, most beautifulest lady that has called the station tonight.

SHEILA: Maybe not, you have to ask him.

Wha is you boyfriend's name?

SHEILA: Sorrel.

Sorry? Your boyfriend's name is Sorry?

SHEILA: No, Sorrel, like the drink, Sorrel. It's a nickname.

De man name Sorry? What is a pretty lady like you doing with a man call Sorry?

SHEILA: No, Sorrel, Sorrel.

I tell you Sheila dear I am so sorry about that.

SHEILA: Sorrel!

Do you mind if I ask you on a date?

SHEILA: You tryin to get me in trouble Mister Morris?

I don't wanna get you in trouble I just wanna get you telephone number. Ha! Ha! Ha! Tiger Style Baby, Worries and Trouble! Send some greetins out there for me Sheila.

SHEILA: Can you play that Johnny King song for me?

Johnny King! Soca Business! Sheila Dear are you Bajian?

SHEILA: No sir, Guyana.

Guyanese Massive! I'll see if I can't find some Johnny King for you. Thanks for callin in Sheila from Brooklyn!

SHEILA: Ok, Bye. Love you Sorrel!

Yes people, the man says lookout, lookout, lookout Calling all Trinidadian Massive! All Tobagonian! All Bajian, all St. Vincent, all St. Lucian, all Grenadian, all Antiguan, all Guyanese, all Caribbean Massive! The man says This night! Tonight! Friday night! Soca meets Calypso over there at the Golden Pavillion over there on Empire Boulevard in Brooklyn the man says it gonna be HOT! Admission is only Ten Smackers in this budget deficit time. Security Fort Knox style. The man says is gonna be better than cook food!

And speakin of cook food people. The records played for you in this fifteen-minute segment is brought to you by Angie's West Indian Restaurant and Bakery over there at 135-16 Church Avenue between Nostrand and Rogers Avenues and that's in Fun City Brooklyn. Servin up the freshest and most superb in West Indian Delicacies. We're talkin about Escoveiched Fish, Cow Foot Soup, all Roti done up just like your grandmother cook it Fresh! Tell them you heard it from me the Caribbean Tiger and you get free Beef Patty. Mmm! Vaughn Morris Is A First Class Tiger, Vaughn Morris Is A First Class Tiger.

MADMAN

[It's three in the morning at a Jamaican Dancehall spot in the Bronx. One of the live acts for the night, Madman, sporting a leather calabash and sunglasses, pops out of the dark into a spotlight and charms the stage with his romantic ragamuffin stylee.]

Yes! A . . . a . . . Ahh! Love You. I want to welcome all de people to de number one night spot inna Bronx. Act Three In The Tropics place. Yes. Fresh and Hot. I want to introduce myself to de people dem. Me a de Madman. Dem a call me Madman beca me mad inna me head, but seh me na crazy. Fresh and Hot! Me a de number one dancehall entertainer fe de people dem. I want to big up all de people who come all the way to check me out tonite. Big up to the Bronx people dem. People from de Brooklyn, de Queens, de Manhattan. New Jersey, Go Home! Staten Island Stay Away! Yes! How many people dem out dere make alotta money? Wole up yu han you make money! Come wid it selector . . . Me bal- Me make de money, ya know me make de money . . . Cease selector! Fresh and hot! Mea de Madman. Me na ramp, me na joke, me na skin teeth! Me always come 100% Gold Ring, Gold Chain, Gold Tooth, Bally Shoe! And whe eva me go, you know seh me haffe mek a ton a cash. Donald Trump celebrity cyaant touch me bwoy! I love you! I blow a kiss to you! Hug an kiss to each and every person. Special big big super hug an kiss to de gyal wid de fat an healthy body. Me say me love de fat body gyal.

Some People

Me na wan no skinny gyal, ca de toothpick gyal mussee garbage pan way. Wole up yu han you don hav a Slim Fast Diet now! Huh! Mea de numba one! I want all my fans to reach out and touch me tonight, because I goin be fresh and hot, like magic inna dancehall place. Touch me, you can touch me, touch me. You cyaant touch me. I am too hot. Me a de Hot Potato. Yes selector, beca you know seh from me born outta me moda belly, me know me is fresh and hot every time. How many people dem out dere you can keep a riddim? How many White people dem can keep a riddim? Not a one, not a one . . . You can keep a riddim? Follow me . . . [audience participation]

All first row people. All second row people. All third row people. Fresh. This is a participatory performance process. We ago do this fe about three hours now. Follow me . . .

Me a de Madman, me deh from New York City

Me nah ramp me na joke me na skin teeth-people don tes me

Me hav de style an de class an de personality

Me seh me walk pon street, people admire me

Alla de pretty gyal dem rush me inna hurry

Deh wan fe me cash an fe me jewelry

Eve-ry gyal wan to have my baby

Beca me terrible good lookin an me neva ugly

When me pickiny, me usee entertainer

Me usee chat lyric pon de corner

Beg likkle money from rich foreigna

Now me big bad, make a million dolla

Me hav one Toyota an one Maxima

One home New York, one home Jamaica

Champagne, Bubble Bath, Leather Sofa

With Gold Chain Pon Me Neck An Ring Pon Me Finga!

Cease! Bally Shoe! Round of applause fe de people dem. I love you. Hug an kiss to each an every person. Me a de Madman! Always come 100% Gold Ring, Gold Chain, Gold Tooth. Bally Shoe! Hug an kiss! Love You!

KAZMIERCZACK

[*Kazmierczack, handyman for this tenement building, comes to fix the stove in a tenant's apartment in the afternoon. He knocks on the imaginary door. No one answers. He sees a familiar face down the hall and waves.*]

Anya! Yakshemash! Viglondash bardzo wadnye gishe . . . Dopshe, dopshe.

[*She leaves. He tries the door again.*]

Halo! Is Kazmierczack! ..Halo. Kazmierczack. ..Halo eh, You something broke? Something you break? Something you always never very good? Ah! Kazmierczack, Rama-me, coming you fix. Ah, I fix. Thank You.

[*He enters the apt.*] What you break? Sink good, no good? Ah, good. I no fix . . . Ah? Cook? Never coming hahh? Only bad? Never this ahh? I look. Maybe you many cook. ..Ah, is no good. I fix. You many cook? Many cook you? You Chodak cook? Chodak. Eh, chodak. Dook dook dook. Ah, Chicken. Never chicken cook? Ah. Is good. You bread cook? Bread? Ah, is good. America, bread, good. Never bad dollar money bread. Ah, America-dollar, My Poland-zwodzhe. Dollar, zwodzhe is all mmm, eh. You wish pay money bread this one Key Food. You maybe, Halo—can I please one bread? This Thank You Very Key Food Bread You. My Poland you wish pay money bread, never good dollar. My Poland you wish pay money this, automobile, good dollar, you wish pay money bread, bad dollar, is no good . . . You look? [*He motions to the steel putty in his hand.*] After take ten, eleven minute put ahh, after make aghh! Is go aghh, metal, pa! Is good. ..You work? What you work? ..Teacher? Oh, I know teacher . . . this . . . small people. You teacher good money? ..Bad. My wife teacher, this small people. My Poland, teacher good money. America teacher no money. Is no good. Never money teacher, all small people is go ahhh! Is bad. ..You cat? Cat. Eh, cat . . . meow . . . Ah, cat. Kazmierczack never look you cat. Only look you cat . . . box. Cat go ahhh. Ah. ..Two cat? Oh, bad. My wife cat. One, small. Maybe, one week, after Kazmierczack finish this work, me go this home, for small ten eleven minute sleep me. This shoe go ahh for ah. Cat, one, small, my wife, coming this-ehha. Only maybe this one week, cat only always never very good. This one week, cat every ahhhh. Only ahh. Ah, throw! Throw! This cat is throw, my shoe. After Kazmierczack finish this sleep. Me, go this-ah. Look shoe. Ey, cat! Why you throw this my shoe? Cat look me, Ahh Never this shoe throw nothing me you this. Is no good. ..Ok, I fix. Ah, maybe you stop fifteen sixteen minute for hwooh. After come metal. Ok I fix. You this bread cook, you this Chodak cook. Ah, Chicken cook. Ok, Thank You. Dozobachenia. [*He exits.*]

FLOE

[*Floe, a cool sixteenish, sits with two friends and beats hip-hop into the wooden box to supply the music for his rhyme.*]

It's the mack motherfuckin, Daddy

Never catch me drivin a caddy

I prefer like a 190E

Imported all the way from Germany

It's the F to the L to the O to the E

I tantalize to tickle your throat like Tetley Tea

I terrorize, stuff tough trash talkers and bluff tykes

Twist the wrist to grab the microphone and I wear Nikes

Color green, style hi-top, to flex the hip-hop

Born to rip the shop and rock the spot like nonstop, yo . . .

My rhymes are fat, fresh, dumb, dope, down and groovy

Some People

I'm terminatin suckas like Schwarzenegger in that movie

Sucker Emcees I consume, my rhymes boom

I knew I was dope walkin out my mother's womb

I'll kick you in the head with my Tims, so I could squoosh ya

See ya on the street punk, word up I'll mush ya

I'm not a pusher, flowin like a gusher

A fucked up motherfucker and I live inside Flatbush-uh

I'm makin dynamite explode, I'm launchin rockets

I robbed George Jetson, stuck up Spaceley Sprockets

My pockets stay fat, with pictures of the presidents

I'm ricochet-bing-bing rockin rhymes for all ya residents

Of Brooklyn, Queens, Manhattan and the Bronx

You paid your fifteen dollars, yo I coulda got yaw'll comps

Everytime I rhyme I leave mikes twisted and bent

Never been to Riker's Island but I almost went

I'm out there murfin, not Papa Smurf and

Foamin like a Nerf and yeah, I fucked your girlfriend

I smoke suckas mad fast just like the crack

I drop more fuckin bombs than Bush did on Iraq

I'm stacked and stacked, drink a forty of Similac

Never call me wack because yo, kid I pack

A pistol, so it's no use holdin your crystal

I'll shoot ya point blank in the head, then fuck your sister

I'll throw ya down and step on your head just like a Ring Ding

Beat ya ass worse than they did in the Rodney King thing

The rhymes I hit ya with boy, they aint no duds

The microphone's the trigger and boom, I'm droppin Scuds

Yeah, and ya don't stop, keep on till the break of dawn and . . .
[*Freestyle*]

[*To his boys*] Ah yeah you like that, you like that. I fucked it up though. I made up the part about the Scuds yesterday. I was like tryin to you know, end on some boom shit but at the same time relate it to like current events . . . What? You can't have the sample after my verse man. You already got it after his verse. Cause, that shit is mad redundant. You don't know what the fuck you talkin about . . .

Aight fine, then have the sample after my verse but then you can't have it after his . . . Oh my god, shut the fuck up. We aint even make the demo yet. Wait till we drop the demo, get a record deal, then when you got cash in your pocket you'll shut the fuck up then. Cause people are gonna listen to it and be like, that shit is mad redundant. You do get money, cause you know you get a advance right? Like I heard Wu-Tang Clan got like two hundred-fifty thousand dollars each before the record even came out! Each yo, each, each! But watch, this be just the motherfucker to like, take that money, and go buy like a five hundred bag of Buddha and ten hookers and shit. ..Cause you're stupid. Hey yo, I get that money, I'm goin to college in two seconds, yup. Cause otherwise they just look at you like another dumb rapper and shit. You got a degree in your pocket, niggas give you respect. For real, I'm gonna roll up like Harvard or Yale or some shit. Yo there's mad honeys at them schools too yo. ..Nah bee, you don't need SAT's to get into that shit. Nah yo. I roll up in Harvard, a hundred thousand dollars in my pocket, they be like, aight you in, you in. Trust me. They be like, Oh Hello, Welcome and shit.

..What? You don't know what the fuck you're talkin about. You can't even rhyme for shit anyway. Aha! ..My mother can't rhyme? Yo, your mother's so stupid, she climbed up a tree cause she tryin to be branch manager. ..Yo, your mother's so dumb, she got stabbed in a shoot-out. ..Hah? ..Oh, why you wanna go there man? . . . I'm sayin, you dis my moms all you want, but you don't talk about my girl, that's different. ..I know she aint my girl no more, that's not the point though. Yo we broke up, you don't even know the whole story. Nah I'm sayin, she wanna go roll with some other kid cause he got money in his pocket. That's aight though. Cause wait till we get this record deal and I got money in my pocket, you know she gonna be callin me up like, ring ring, hi, I'm sorry. I'll be like, word? Click. ..Nah, actually I can't say that. Cause she aint really the type to do that shit. See, that's why I can't dis her even though we broke up. I mean out of all the girls I been with, I be like, seeya! But it's like that's the first girl that like, I don't know. I think honestly I could say like . . . I don't know, some shit.

Nah! I'm serious! It's like, even just being with her, we don't even have to be doing nothing, we just be sitting there. Plus she be schooling me, cause you know she's in college right? She's gonna be a sophomore at Hunter next semester. ..Black and Puertorican studies. So I'm sayin, it's like we just be chilling or whatever. And all of the sudden she'll drop the bomb of knowledge on me. Like check this out, there was this whole civilization, livin on the islands in the Caribbean, mad hundred thousand years before the Europeans came over and fucked that whole shit up. They was called Tainos.

They had a whole civilization, architecture, medicine, culture. ..Tainos. ..You aint never heard of no fuckin Tainos. This nigga aint never heard of Fritos talkin bout you heard of that shit. I'm sayin though. Shit was just different with her. ..That too though. It's like, even when I was fuckin her. Ah, see I can't even say that cause it wasn't like fuckin. It was like, we was making love or some shit. ..Shut up. Stop laughing. Your mother's so fat she jumped in the air and got stuck, shut the fuck up. Nah, shut the fuck up stop laughing though. I'm saying, I'm gonna tell you this cause it still be buggin me out to this day. This happened like once right? ..I'm not saying I fucked her once, but listen. You

Some People

know when you be gettin busy and like you get all into the moment and shit? Like you get all hot and sweaty and you get into the smells, like you be smelling her neck and shit. You know, you be like, ah lemme smell your neck? So, I'm saying like one time, we was all in it. And I had closed my eyes and this shit had come over me like I can't even explain it. Like in here, and I had like almost started like, cryin and shit. I mean I'm not saying I was crying. I'm saying like, aight. The only thing I could compare it to, is remember last summer we went to Action Park? ..Nah, aight bad example, bad example.

I'm sayin, you ever been on a airplane? ..So you know you be on a airplane and you hit turbulence and the plane drops. And your stomach goes like this, but the rest of your body goes like this. It's like you're separating and you feel like . . . I'm saying, so they got that water slide at Action Park, and when you go down the slide you be like, wahh. I'm not sayin down there, I'm saying like in here. Never mind man. Nah, forget it, shut up, you're stupid. Watch in like five years, she'll be some college professor, and we'll be on tour at her school. And we'll run into each other and be like, ching! Nah yo, let me shut up man. I be sounding all sentimental like Sally Jeffrey Rafael and shit. Yo, kick your verse man, kick your verse! Ya big, can't rhyme for your life . . . What? Yo, your mother got no arms on Wheel Of Fortune talkin bout, Big Money, Big Money! [*Floe pounds the box to his homeboy's imaginary verse.*]

BILL

[A straight-outta-Jersey pseudo-yuppie with a Jeep runs up to his friend's apartment with him for a would-be two minutes. Bill talks while his friend struggles with the many locks on the door.]

Alright but just for two minutes because my jeep is double-parked downstairs and I don't want to get tickets. Can I tell you what your problem is? And this is your problem because I know because I'm very good at telling things about people. You, you don't pay attention to things that are going on around you. It's like you're in this shell. You're like this turtle, you know, crawling along the grass in your shell and bombs are dropping like five centimeters away from you. And you, you're in lala land. You're like, la la. Can I give you an example? Let me give you a perfect example. Did you watch Ted Koppel last week? Ok well if you would've watched, you would've known that there's little nine year olds running around the street with guns, selling crack to babies for sex. You think I'm exaggerating? If you would've watched, you would've known. You also would've known, get this. There's some guy, he killed all these hookers right? You know, prostitutes? Killed them. But this is the thing, there are all these people and they're in this rage that he shouldn't have killed them. Lemme tell you something, if he didn't kill them they would've wound up spreading AIDS to half the people in this country. ..Because this is a very serious issue of our time and it affects us all indirectly.

..Ok, I'll give you a perfect example. Let's say, some guy he makes a mistake. Not me, but some guy. He goes and uses a prostitute, right? She gives him AIDS, cause she's got AIDS, she gives it to him, he goes home to his wife, he gives it to her, she has no idea. Are you following the progression of the story? Then they get a divorce, because of course they're gonna get a divorce because why is the guy with the . . . Anyway, she's out there, you know on the single scene, whatever you wanna call it. I'm thirty-five years old, I'm a single man. I meet her, she gives me AIDS, I'm dead. You're asking how it affects me? ..Use a condom? I'm thirty-five years old, I think I'm a little old to use a condom, anyway you're missing the whole point of the story. Listen, I thought we're coming up here for two minutes so you could shave, this is turning into a whole ordeal here with getting into your apartment. What's with the five locks on your door, what are we in Harlem? Heh . . . It's a joke, you got five locks on your door, you know, Harlem, it's all these people up there? ..Alright, so it's not funny, so now you're a Black Panther all of the sudden? Jesus, it's a joke. Mr. Medeco here. You make me very uncomfortable sometimes.

[*Bill enters apartment.*] Oh, this is nice. ..I said this is nice, your place. How much do you pay for this? ..Not bad. Who's the guy that owns the building? The same guy that owns the building on the corner? What's his name? ..Mohammed? Is he Moroccan? ..But is he Moroccan? ..Yeah but is he Moroccan though? No, I bet he's Moroccan. Because all the Moroccans, they bought up all the real estate, from the Jews. ..No, yes, trust me. They did a whole in-depth report on MacNeil Lehrer, I saw the whole thing. You didn't know the Jews are going poor? Not just that they had to sell . . . Trust me, my friend who's Jewish. He wanted to get for his daughter . . . what do you call it when they get their own . . . her own phone line. He couldn't get it for her, that's all I'm saying. Anyway that's not the point of the story. The point of the story is that all the Moroccans bought up all the real estate, and all the Baskin-Robbins. And I don't know this just because I watch TV and I'm socially aware, paying attention unlike you—you're in lala land, but I know this from empirical observation. I was in a Baskin-Robbins last month and I'm standing there paying for the cone, and I ask the guy his name. You know I'm always taking advantage of these little small-talk opportunities, you get to know people really well. So the guy says Mohammed. ..The guy's Moroccan, so he's Moroccan, Libyan, Hindu, Iraqi. They're all connected. They're all in the same little boat there.

Let me ask you something, do you watch Dan Rather? From now on, you have to watch Dan Rather just for educational purposes. Because on Dan Rather, you get the whole complete story. Let me explain something to you. They got this whole Shiite cult, the Buddhists right? And the thing is they name them all Mohammed, so they can't tell the difference between each other. It's like brainwashing. They're brainwashing them into thinking that they're all this one common organism floating around the earth, and they're gonna take over other organisms, and the other ones are innocent law-abiding countries, like ours. I mean they didn't say that exactly on Dan Rather but you could figure it all out. The Shiites are sort of like the Moonies, it's all interwoven. Anyway that's not the point, the point is just be careful there's not a bomb in your building. You think these guys got real estate on their minds? I'm thinking not . . . Where'd you get this, Ikea? ..This table thing here, I thought it was Ikea. Heh.

Some People

Listen, hurry up because if I got tickets on my Jeep you're paying for them. Hey you know I'm thirty-five right? Yeah, I turned thirty-five last week. ..Thank you thank you. Anyway, you know I'm old enough to be president, right? You know what I'd do if I was president? You know, to solve all the problems, hatred, racism, killing, stuff? Now keep in mind I'm not prejudice or anything, I'd teach everybody how to speak English. Because that's the problem. I mean, if you don't speak English, how are we supposed to communicate for, you know, peace? Let me give you a perfect example. The other day I finish work, I'm hungry, I feel like having Chinese food. So I go to the Chinese take-out in my neighborhood, I order what I always order. Four fried chicken wings, it comes with a small roast pork fried rice. So this day, me, I'm feeling hungrier than normal, so I order a large roast pork fried rice instead of a small, you know? I'll pay for it. So I say to the guy, can I have a large instead of a small? So the guy goes yeah, like he understands what I'm saying. Mistake Number One, the guy doesn't know what the hell I'm saying. You wanna hear Mistake Number Two? Me, I'm looking out the window making sure my Jeep isn't getting ripped off by, you know, crackhead murderers in the street. Meanwhile, I should be watching, who knows what the hell they're putting in my food? Poison, whatever . . . You don't know what they put in, they have their little jars of stuff next to the woks. So that's not even the thing. This is the thing. The guy goes to put it in the bag with the duck sauce and everything. Get this, he puts it in the bag behind the counter. So you can't really see what he's putting in the bag, it could be a bomb . . . Ep, you're laughing? You're very unaware.

Can I just tell you, *20/20* did a whole four-part series on bombings and Barbara was explaining that these bombs went off, and nobody would have ever guessed that there was a bomb. ..Then why do they put it in the bag behind the counter then? They got a whole top of the counter, the top of the counter's clean. Everything is behind the counter, behind the counter . . . They're very sneaky. So the moral of the story is, I take the bag, I drive all the way home, four blocks. Meanwhile, I could blow up on the way home. I sit down, I take off my shoes, I turn on the TV. I wanna relax, you know. I worked hard all day, I don't know about *these* people. I open the bag, they gave me a small . . . A small roast pork fried rice, are you listening to the story? Alright. So me, I'm angry. I'm flustered. I'm looking into the bag and it's like looking into this tunnel of frustration and anger. So I put it back in the bag, I drive all the way back, four blocks, so now it's eight blocks I've driven for this thing already.

I walk in to the guy, see now the guy's not there anymore. Now it's his sister, or his mother, or his wife, his aunt . . . they're all in the family there . . . Because I know, because I know. So I say to her, look, I ordered a large, you gave me a small. So she says, what? Already we're having miscommunication. So I tell her, I-want-a-large. She says, $2.50. I say, no, no, hello, before, earlier . . . I'm trying to think of all the possible adjectives, I'm like a thesaurus. You know, prior to the time when I'm standing before you here now, I already, then, ordered a large. You made a mistake. You know, I mean I'm a man, I'm thirty-five years old, I'm not a kid. I want service, you know? So she's going, dut dut dut dut dut dut dut dut dut. Like I'm supposed to understand what she's saying? She's supposed to understand *me*, thank you! So then she turns to her brother or her husband or her uncle . . . Because just trust me, they are, I know the people in my neighborhood. And she's saying something to

him very fast. So I'm trying to listen to what she's saying, she's telling him to blow me up for all I know. So then cause I'm listening, cause I'm a listener, I hear her say this thing and I recorded it in my brain and I want to do it for you so shut off the water. She says, something something, and then she says, "beaow." What does mean? That's not a normal sound.
..Because I went to college I have a Master's Degree in business, thank you, I think I know a little something about languages if you give me the benefit of the doubt.

Look, the point of the story is this, these people have got to go through some sort of assimilation program before they come to this country so they can, a) learn how to speak English, and b) learn how to function like normal human beings, like us.
..Because how are you gonna run a business and not speak English? Look at the guy who owns the 7-Elevens, he's from India, he learned how to speak it. Look at the American Indians, they learned to speak it when they came over here. But see these people, they come from out of nowhere, and in twenty-four hours they get a license to open a restaurant. That's like giving a woman, a license . . . to fix trucks. I mean not that I'm saying women can't fix trucks, it's just . . . I don't really know what I'm saying actually. The bottom line is this, if you took all these people, from the cleaning people, the nannies, and the maintenance people, the housekeepers, and the kitchens, the guys that work at the place where I get my Jeep washed. If you took all of them and you sent them back to all of their little terrorist countries, we wouldn't have all this suffering here and just, things wouldn't be as hard.

..Trust me, I'll get somebody to wash it, there'll be somebody. Oh, you have a cat. I didn't see before. It must have just come out from wherever it was. That's funny how all of the sudden they just decide to run out of nowhere. You don't seem like the cat-type. You know it's my favorite animal? Is it a Persian? . . . I bet it's name is Mohammed. Hi kitty cat. Hiya ya big cutie. Ooh too too. What are you looking at? What are you doing? Where are you going? Ooh too too. Moo moo mama. Come here cutie. I'm gonna get you. I'm gonna get you . . . Oh I got you. Oh. I. Got. You. Oh you're so heavy you little small kitty cat. Let's go look in the mirror. Oh, look in that mirror. Look. In. That. Mirror. Who's that guy behind you? I don't know. Some guy. Gimme that paw. Gimme that paw. Lemme see that paw. How you doing? I'm ok. Hah. Oh ribbit ribbit. Moo. Gobble gobble. Meow . . . Ep. Look at all this shit I got all over me now. Listen, I'm going downstairs. I got a hundred and fifty tickets on my Jeep already, or they towed it . . . Trust me they're giving out tickets. I just read, they hired all these *whatever* me-ermaids, all they do is hand out tickets all day. Because I read it. What do you think they write it for nothing? These guys they got this whole thing connected to those hate groups that were on *60 Minutes*. What they do these guys, they see my Jeep, they see the Jersey plate, automatically they assume that I'm White. I mean I am, but that's not the point. The point is that they think that Jersey's all White people. Let me tell you it's not. You come to my neighborhood, I gotta get five locks on my door. Listen I'll see ya downstairs. [*Bill exits.*]

BLANCA

[Blanca, a young twenty-something office worker stops by her friend's house to borrow shoes.]

Listen Lisette, lemme borrow your shoes? The short black ones. ..No because Manny gets off Footlocker in twenty minutes and I have to take the bus. ..But I can't be looking ugly in the bus. ..So find them! Don't stress me more alright. My life is already stressed enough, can I tell you? The other day right? I was at Manny's house, and we was fooling around, and like you know how guys be getting all shy like when they wanna say something really important but they don't say it? Or like they say it, but like their voices be getting all low so you can't hear what they saying? So he was doing that right, and like I don't be playing that. I was like, hello-excuse-me-I-can't-hear-you-what-you-saying, right?

So I figure he's doing that because he wants to ask me to marry him cause already we been together one year nine months seventeen days and he aint asked me nothing. So I look, and he got this thing behind his back and I figure it's a Hallmark card or something saying like, hello Blanca how you doing I love you will you marry me. Instead, he got a condom right? ..Right? So I was like, excuse me who's that for? He was like, that's for us. I was like, excuse me, I do not think that's for us. But he goes, no we have to use it, because he said that he had seen some thing in like Channel 13 or something, like some thing. He goes, no you have to be careful you don't know what's out there. I was like, excuse me, I know what's out there, I'm talking about what's in here, right? I was like, you aint sticking no fucking rubber shit up inside me I don't know who touched it. You might as well put a rubber glove and do some Spic and Span in that shit, cause I aint having that. ..No cause, one year nine months seventeen days we been together, now he comes to me with it? *Now* he thinks I'm dirty? I aint fucking dirty.

And he thinks like I don't know nothing. Like he thought that I thought that you could get it from mosquitoes. Plus it aint like I just met him. I know his whole family, his parents, his sisters. They're nice people. If I would have got something, I would have got it one year nine months seventeen days ago, right? ..No, we talked about it but you think we used it? Ps. We started fooling around, I was like, you seen *this* in Channel 13? He was like, no. I was like, mmm-hmm.

..Not those, the black ones you wore last Friday! The short ones with the bows on it. I'm telling you though, Manny be driving me crazy sometimes for the dumb reasons. Like, you know Manny's father's Puertorican and his mother's Spanish. So he's Puertorican right. And he's dark and his last name is Sorullo. So when people ask him, he always says Sorulo. Cause he says he wants to work in business in Wall Street, and that nobody wants to hire a Sorullo. So I be telling him, Manny, that's your last name, you can't do that. And he be getting angry at me like, That's my last name, that's how it's pronounced! And like, you got it easier than me Blanca cause you're lighter than me, cause you're a woman. And I'm like, excuse me, I'm

Puertorican too, right? So it was the Puertorican Day Parade, and I had gotten us these T-shirts with the Puertorican flag in the front, and in the back there's a little Coquí and it says Boricua and Proud. So you would think that he would be like, oh thank you Blanca that's so sweet I love you, right? Instead he starts screaming. I'm not wearing this shit! I can't believe you got me this! It's ugly! I was like, excuse me, it's not ugly. So he puts on a Ralph Lauren shirt. I was like, Manny, you think somebody's hiring you for Wall Street at the Puertorican Day Parade? So he goes to me, Look Blanca, I might be Puertorican, but I don't have to walk around looking like one . . . I was like, excuse me. You think that people think that you Swedish? You Puertorican. I couldn't believe it. It's like, he wants to wear a condom, but not a T-shirt.

..Not those ugly heels, the short ones with the bows. ..So find them, don't stress me more! It's like I be nice to people and they be having temper tantrums. You're like Lemington. You know my roommate Lemington, right? . . . I know, his name is Lemington, that's weird right? So you know he's gay right? And you know if you see Lemington, you be like, oh my god this guy is gay. But if you see his boyfriend, you be like, oh my god this guy is not gay. Cause he's like six foot and all muscular. Like when I first had seen him I was like, mmm. Like that, right? But he's gay. And they're not only gay, they're Black and gay. Can you believe that? I couldn't believe that. ..No, cause they don't look like those guys from *In Living Color*. At all. But you know I don't care cause I'm very liberal. But I think that his boyfriend be beating him cause one day Lemington had a cut right here, and I seen those signs in the subway that like if you're gay and your lover beats you call that number . . . right . . . whatever.

So we be getting along, except this one morning I'm getting ready to go to work. It's like seven-thirty in the morning and I'm sitting there eating breakfast, I look up and he's wearing my skirt. So I was like, Lemington what you doing with my skirt? He was like, That's your skirt? I was like, yes that's my skirt, Lemington, where you got it? He goes, In the closet. I was like, well that would happen to be my closet, which would happen to be in my room, so that would happen to be, Ding! My skirt, right? I was like, Lemington you can't be wearing my skirt. So he starts crying, right? And he's like, Fine, I won't wear it! And I can't have him crying in my house at seven-thirty in the morning cause then the neighbors be thinking like *I'm* beating him or something right. So we had gotten over it right. Except that he be leaving me these pamphlets all over the house. Like in the dishes he puts them, in the freezer. So, should I go to get a ice cube, I'll read a pamphlet. Meanwhile I got frozen pamphlets in the freezer. It's this one pamphlet, it's called, Getting To Know Your Body. It's these drawings of these women, looking at themselves, in you know, there, with instructions. Excuse me, but I don't need to be looking there. For what? It's money in there? Plus, what if somebody comes over and they go to get a ice cube, they'll be thinking that I'm looking in there with instructions like, what's this? He thinks that I'm like one of these women that doesn't know nothing about her body and goes and does whatever. [*She puts on some lipstick.*]

But he's sweet though, he got me this cute shirt with all these pictures of famous womens on it. Clara Barton, Nefertiti, Mother Teresa is on the shirt. And he gives it to me and he goes to me, Rejoice in your womanhood Blanca, be good to yourself cause you're a warrior. I was like . . . ? This is some Black gay thing or something? He called me a warrior. I picture myself like running through the jungle with a machine gun like, lookout it's Blanca coming!

But the thing is, now he got this little dog right? And a) he don't be feeding it, so the dog be eating my curtains, now I don't have no curtains people could just be looking at me naked through the window. And b) he don't walk it. So the dog be shitting all in my house. And let me tell you, I don't know what the dog be shitting because it got nothing to eat but curtains. It's like little curtain shits is in the floor. The other day I'm getting ready to go to work and I get out the shower in my towel, I step in this little macadamia nut shit. So he goes, Wipe it. So I wipe it, I took a Bounty but I don't have time to go back in the shower and scrubbing shit out my foot twenty-four hours. So I go to work. People at work are like, Ooh you smell like shit. And when I explain to them that, excuse me, I do not smell like shit naturally, but I happened to *step* in shit. They're like, Oh you stepped in shit? You must be stupid then. And I'll tell you right now, I can't have people calling me stupid cause I aint stupid.

..No, I wanna kick him out, but then he'll think it's cause he's gay. I mean it's not that he's gay that his dog shits in the floor, it's that he's irresponsible. Things are so complicated. Plus I think he got AIDS too, cause he's all skinny. ..Yeah Manny's skinny too, but Manny's just skinny. Lemington's gay and skinny alright? But them people be getting that shit anyway right? ..They do though right? ..Right. You got them? Finally, gimme. I hope they fit. I'm telling you, you know what is it? [*Blanca puts on the shoes and checks herself in the mirror.*] I think my life is stressed because I have to learn to be nice to myself. Cause if you think about it, nobody's being nice to me. You included. But listen, I have to go because you making me late. And these shoes are too tight but I'm wearing them. And let me tell you something. If Manny comes to me with that whole condom thing again, I'm gonna tell him like this, You think I'm dirty? Who do you think I am? Do you even know who you are?

AL CAPÓN

[*Al Capón is a fast-paced disc-jockey and radio personality. He is almost the Latinamerican/Spanish-Speaking counterpart of Caribbean Tiger. The stage is dimly lit and he races from time and weather to live advertisements with quick Merengue interludes.*]

Andando! Holy Moly Guacamole mis amigos. Tenemos las doce y treinta minutos y estámos con el super exito de Toño Rosario! Wow! Yo soy Adalberto Capón, mejor conocido a ustedes, Al Capón. Aquí estoy en tu SuperPoderosa FM 99. Holy Moly Guacamole, la temperatura afuera está de 27 grados entónces, cuídanse mucho que no cogan gripe porque hay muchas mongas afuera que coger! Ok ok ok. Cambio! [*Music*]

Este Sábado el 2000 Club presenta directamente de Santo Domingo la capital del Merengue, Jossie Esteban y La Patrulla 15. Las mujeres entran Gratis! Gratis! Gratis! Ántes de las once. Otra vez, Jossie Esteban y La Patrulla 15 Este Sábado en el 2000 Club en la calle 177 y Broadway en el alto Manhattan! El 2000 Club!

Ok ok ok. Este segmento de música de quince minutos está presentado por KoolAid. KoolAid KoolAid KoolAid. Disponible en todos los sabóres que te encantarán. Como SuperCherry, SuperGrape, SuperStrawberry y FunkyFruit! Ok ok ok. KoolAid KoolAid KoolAid. Andando! [*Music*]

Some People

Este Fín de Semana en el Gigantic Tomato Supermarket en Brentwood, Long Island! La SuperVenta del Siglo Holy Moly! Muslos de Pollo Shady Brook Farms—99 centavos por libra! Plantanos SuperVerdes—nueve por un dólar! SweetPotato SweetPotato Marca Gran Batata—79 centavos por libra! Holy Moley I Can't Believe It! Este Fín de Semana en el Gigantic Tomato Supermarket en Brentwood, Long Island!

Ok Ok Ok mis amigos aquí estámos en la capital del mundo, Nueva York. Y estámos con, Happy Birthday To You, Happy Birthday To You, Happy Birthday Dear . . . Isabel Santiago del Bronx. Happy Birthday To You. Ok ok ok. Muchas Felicidades a usted Isabel Santago del Bronx de su esposo Manny Santiago, allá en el Bronx también por supuesto.

Ok ok ok. Si tú eres good looking, o si tú eres looking good, call me baby. Porque yo no soy alcapurria, yo soy Al Capón, aquí en tu SuperPoderosa Hot FM 99. Holy Moly Guacamole Mis Amigos! Andando! [*Music*]

DORIS

[*Doris, a mother of one in her fifties, is in her kitchen, using her power-tool, the phone, to communicate with some people, while her husband fixes something in another room.*]

Will you shush! ..So shah! Martin, the guy is coming in five minutes. So leave the thing alone! In five minutes he'll be here and he'll fix the whole thing . . . I know the phone is ringing, I'm letting it ring. ..So let me let it ring!

..Hello? Who is this? Who? Oh, Hi! How are you? No, what are you interrupting? You're interrupting nothing. Uy, no, no. I'm sitting here, I'm— What wire Martin? What wire? I'm supposed to know what wire you're talking about? Oh, that wire, sure. Keep futzing with the wire and blow yourself up. You're not blowing me up!

..No, I'm fine. Martin's fine. David's fine. Yeah, in fact, I'm supposed to call my sonny boy in five minutes so I'll talk quick. No, no he's fine. How's your daughter? Gonna marry to who? Not the same Nigerian guy? Does she love him? So, she loves him and she'll be happy and they'll be happy. Listen, did she make sure he's all tested with all whatever he needs with shots and everything? No, I'm just saying, because especially with he's from Africa, she should make sure cause I saw in the *Times*. ..How terrible. Isn't it? ..He's a doctor the guy? And he's from Nigeria? Eh, well still. ..No, he doesn't see her anymore. Eh, Roz, to tell you the truth, I had a bad feeling about her when I first met her. She's a sweet girl, and she's attractive, but there was something creepy about her. She had a creepy aura. Anyway. Did I tell you what he's doing now my son? Oh Roz, he goes with this group of people and they go into all the bad neighborhoods, and I gotta tell ya, I am so . . . Yeah, I think it's like the Peace Corps, but in New York. Who? David? Hold on, let me ask . . .

Martin! Does David get insurance with the job? . . . David your son. Does he get insurance with the job, the thing with the . . . Never mind, you're not understanding me . . . You're not understanding me, never mind! Listen, I'll ask him when I'll call him. Listen mamala, I gotta go darling ok? I'll call you back after. Ok, bye.

[*She clicks the phone only to make another call.*] Martin! How do I do the memory with the phone, I forgot? The memory, for David, I know I put for number one, but after I do the star button or before? ..The pound button? There's no pound button Martin . . . There's no pound button, I'm looking at the phone! Uhh, I'm doing the star! ..Alright shush, it's ringing! It's ringing and I can't hear! Will you keep with the wires, keep breaking the thing more, more break it!

..Hello David sweetheart, it's your mommyface listen . . . Hello? Hi, you're there? So what are you screening your phone calls, someone's after you? So pick up the phone, it's your mother calling, it's a secret that you're there? Uhh, you make me nervous with this machine, one day I'll call it'll say, Hi this is David I'm not here from they killed me on the train or wherever. Alright, I'm relaxed, I just worry with you in all these . . . uch. Yes David, but not everyone takes the trains by theirself to the South Bronx or wherever. Sure the people that live there, but they're different . . . I mean not that they're different, they're the same as us, everyone is the same, but, alright, never mind, it's just different you don't get it, forget it. You can't take a cab sometimes? So let everybody else take the train, you're not them, you have to do what they do? Alright I'm relaxed.

Anyway boobala what I wanna ask ya . . . Does your job, do they give you health insurance? So you'll pay the ten dollars and you'll have it. How much more? That's ridiculous, are you sure? Alright, so I'll pay it. David, I'm not an extravagant person that I'm saving for a yacht, I'll be happy to pay for it. Or if you want you could go on the plan your father and I have, hold on . . .

Martin! What's the deductible on the insurance? What's that noise? Now you're drilling? What are you drilling? The guy is coming Martin! . . . The deductible! On the Blue Cross, the Blue Cross! . . . That's what I'm asking you how much! . . . Uh, forget it. Forget! It! . . . Listen David honey, we'll call the 1-800, wait, I'm on the phone with David! Hello? *Which* David? Wait one second.

Martin! When the guy comes for the thing, you're staying with him right? ..What do you mean you're going for a walk? Martin, I'm not letting these people into my house I don't know who they are, the minorities or whoever. Uy, you hear this from your father? Where is he walking? In front of a truck he'll walk. ...You're right David, they could be anybody. They could be Jewish, whoever, I'm just saying I'm not staying here alone. While he'll be going for a walk they'll be drilling me in the head for the television. ...Alright. David. I said they didn't have to be minorities. Uy, you're such a mensch, you're a sweetheart, you're very caring, I'm very proud of you, Mmwa! So listen Tatala, do you wanna do with the Blue Cross? What no? Everyone has to have health insurance David. So fine, thirty-six percent of the country doesn't have it, you're not thirty-six percent, you're my son. So David, let the thirty-six percent sit for ten hours waiting in some dirty emergency room somewhere bleeding to death with flies and urine and five hundred sick people with tuberculosis.

My son . . . my son is not gonna sit waiting in some clinic full of people's phlegm all over the floor and everyone's coughing with no air. No David. God forbid. David, God forbid I should be concerned already enough that my son doesn't get shot by some Black kid, *or White kid,* in one of these places, but that he should go to a professional Jewish hospital? . . . I know White people shoot people with guns David, but not on the train. David look, I know I raised you to believe that everyone's equal, and not to be into materials, and to accept people no matter who they are, but David I am your mother and I know you're an adult, but there are some things about reality that you're not understanding. I can't be concerned about my son? I'm not the one yelling, you're yelling! I just want you to be happy and not dead.

David, don't hang up, I want to talk to you. I am proud of you. I brag to all my friends and they all can't believe it. They all say I can't believe it. Is it too much to ask for you to have health insurance? How do you know nothing'll happen? You have a crystal ball? ..David, they'll have one of their riots these people and you'll be the first one they'll shoot. They shoot people David, I read the *New York Times*. Not the *Post*, the *Times*, and I see them. They shoot each other. And let me tell you something David, I feel very bad. I wish these kids didn't have to grow up with all violence and uh, a mess, and my heart goes out to them, it does, but let them shoot each other and not you, that's the way I feel.

..I am not racist David! Don't you dare call me racist! Because if you remember, I let you have all your Black and Puertorican and Iranian friends at your Bar Mitzvah, and I treated them just like I treated your Jewish friends. You wanna see racist? Go read with this guy in the paper, Bloodsuckers he said— I am not a Scared-Liberal-Complaining-Reactionary. What does that mean? When they'll wanna stick you in an oven you'll still defend this guy? You wanna be a another martyr David? You wanna be one of the Jewish kids in Mississippi with the voter registration and they killed them, them and some Black guy? How is it possible for Jews to be prejudice when everyone is prejudice all the time against the Jews? David, we had lots of Black neighbors, before we moved and we got along fine. My friend Roz's daughter Cynthia is marrying a Nigerian guy and he's a doctor! ..No David, the difference is, did I call them Bloodsuckers? I said they shoot people, I didn't call names.

..How am I guilty? I'm guilty of reading the *New York Times*? David, how come you'll never defend the Jews? You're Jewish but you'll never empathize with your own people. What is there to empathize? David, six million. Did you see *Schindler's List*? The Jews are still victims. ..How am I a victim

SOME PEOPLE

in the suburbs in 1994? . . . Not because I have a juicer and an espresso machine makes me a vict— Black people have juicers and espresso makers too! What are you screaming? What bad thing did I do? I did something bad to them? David, I'm not crazy. You ask people if they'll be in these neighborhoods on the train. ..Whatever people. You ask them if they'll defend this guy. The Black kid who's in jail for murder I should defend? For what? Where do you get this from? Why are you so angry, you're not even Black? Why are you angry at your own people? Why are you so angry at me, I'm your mother?

Uy, alright calm down. Stop yelling! Listen to me. Are you still coming to the Seder on Thursday? Your Aunt Barbara's coming and so is your cousin Mark. Mark, the high school principal, gay Mark. And I promise I won't start an argument with you, or Mark. Ok, stop yelling. Are you coming? Well if you don't I'll be very upset. Fine, listen, I'm not angry at you. Are you angry at me? Alright well it's alright I'm your mother. Ok, I love you. Bye . . . Ok stop screaming. Ok bye, Mmwa! [*Doris hangs up the phone.*] Martin . . . I'm going for a walk.

FLEX

[*Flex, nineteen, pants saggin, Timbos draggin, five beepers and a chewstick. He approaches a Chinese take-out restaurant rapping to a song on his Walkman and enters.*]

[*To another customer*] Hey yo, you on line? Aight then. [*Flex looks up at the picture menus on the wall above his head.*] [*To the restaurant guy*] . . . Hey yo I'm still lookin man. Damn man, niggas try to rush me man. [*He takes a moment to ponder his order*] . . . Hey yo Chinaman! Chinaman! Yo Chinese yo! Lemme get Number Seven yo . . . Number Seven! Hey yo I aint look on there yo, I'm lookin right there! Niggas got signs up, don't know what the fuck they got up . . . Hah? Oh Vegetable Lo Mein? Oh I aint see that right there, good lookin. Yo, Vegetable Lo Mein son, small. Small, you know what I'm sayin small? Small! ..Hey yo my man, no mushrooms, no onions in that yo. ..Mushrooms, you know mushrooms? No mushrooms. And no onion. ..Onions! You know what a onion is? I don't eat that shit. I'ma tell you what, I find mushrooms and onions in that shit, you could take that shit back, word up. Hey yo son, how long yo? How long? How long? . . .Right, I'ma be back then.

[*Flex exits to street, rapping to another song and sees his boy.*] Oh shit! Wasup kid? Oh my god! It's the god! It's the god right now. It's that nigga Al! Oh snap. Wasup with you man?

Some People

Goddamn. I aint seen you in the longest time. What you been up to? Word? I hear dat, I hear dat . . . Nuttin man, I'm about to get some food in here right quick, go pick up my little brother from school. Hey yo it's good to see you man. Hey yo check this, I got five beepers kid, you think I'm lyin? Check them shits boy. One, two, three, four, Denent! What you wanna do bout that? These four are like regular, they go like, beep, beep. But this joint right here, this shit go like this, ooh-ooh! Shit's all Disco-style. You should hang out with me for a while and you could hear that shit go off. Hey yo so what you up to lately kid? What you gonna do next year though? ..Get the fuck outta here! Scholarship? See that's cuz you all on that braniac tip.

You thought I forgot. I don't forget shit boy. Remember we used to be in school, and we used to be in the library throwin shit and the teacher used to come by and we'd be like . . . But you was really readin that shit though right. So what you gonna study? You gonna study business right? My man gonna make mad loot in this piece! ..Black History? My man said, Black History yo. Tah ha. This nigga buggin yo! Oh shit, Harriet Tubman, Freedom Fighter, Denent! Your ass gonna be broke as hell beggin in the street and whatnot. Nah, I don't mean to break man, you get mad props for that shit, you get respect. Somebody gotta do that shit right? I'm sayin though, I gotta get that loot son, word is bond. I'm workin this job too, I'm makin bills boy. You want me to make a phone call, you need some extra cash before you take off to school, I could make that phone call for you. These niggas got me workin mad hard. Eight to eight everyday, liftin mad concrete type shit. Cause they buildin this new jail right, so they need construction heads, seventeen a hour kid. I'm makin bank. ..I don't know what I'ma do next year. I think I'ma start a Blunt factory. Nah

I'm playin. I don't smoke that shit god. ..I don't smoke nothin. My lungs is pure yo. This the god right here. I'm sayin how niggas goin buy into that? Let them White kids smoke them drugs man. They make that shit. Yeah right, crack also yo. How Black people gonna smoke somethin that's White? You know mad White people be smokin it too, but you aint seen them on CNN gettin lifted though.

..Right but see, you know what bother me? How one second niggas is like, oh yeah the White man this, White man that. Next second they smokin Phillies tryin to watch David Letterman. Explain that. I'm sayin, one second they like, yeah yeah yeah. Next second they like, yeah yeah yeah. You know what I'm sayin? I'ma tell you like this Al, it's already nuf White kids out here that's tryin to be Black. Peep this, I had to go to Manhattan for this job interview in the Upper West Side. Dead up word to my moms I seen this White kid with Filas, Nautica, Philly Blunt shirt, this kid listenin to X-Clan walkin like this . . . What the fuck is this . . . ? Nigga look like a Weeble-Wabble and shit. ..Yeah yeah! But what you call them White people that don't wash theyself, but they be causin riots and shit? Yeah, them punkrock anarchy niggas right. I seen a bunch of them walkin, all raggedy clothes, rings stickin out they necks and lips. I seen this one Black son in there. I said not the god yo. How a brother gonna be in that shit? Know what I'm sayin?

I be seein wild shit! I see them on TV kid! How a sister gonna sing opera? How a Black man gonna sing backup for some Kenny G? Kenny Rogers? Any one of them Kenny motherfuckers. They all from Alabama and shit, Kentucky. ..Oh that's where your school at? For real? I'ma see you at that school yo.

Some People

I got a scholarship too son. Government-type shit. They gave me five million dollars right. They gonna teach me how to make AIDS yo. I'ma make AIDS Two, AIDS Three, AIDS Four, up to ten. I'ma see how many niggas I could kill yo. Boom! And then cause I'ma be rich right, I'ma buy a penthouse, BMWs, check this yo . . . I'ma own McDonald's, Nike, Levi's, Sony, all that shit. I'ma own Red Lobster. I'ma own that company that make that bomb that we dropped on that nigga Saddam Hussein family. Bpow! I'ma make bank! Then, I'ma see your ass in the street beggin. You know what I'm sayin, you gonna be beggin! Talkin bout Frederick Douglass was a great man, lemme get ten cent. And I'ma be like, Oh whatup Al, remember me? Remember them college days, this and that? And I'ma hit you off with a twenty spot cause you my boy. I'ma get you a job sweepin up one of my Red Lobsters. Aha . . .

What? ..I'ma do what I want son, it's a free country, right? . . . Oh, oh, You gonna tell a Black woman she can't sing opera? . . . Aight then, aight then. He wanna talk garbage right now. This the land of opportunity son, I aint tryin to miss mine yo. This nigga tryin to keep me down now. You sound like this girl yo. I was tryin to talk to this girl, she wanna go see this art exhibit right. So you know me, I got a open mind right. We step up in this museum. Motherfuckers in suits. And it's this art piece on the wall, it got no frame, nails, glue and shit is on the wall. Motherfuckers is like, Mmm yeah, I like that shit. I said straight up, that's some bullshit right there. She go like this in my face son, Maybe if you was more educated you might understand that. I said, What? Hold up now. I'ma go to school so I could understand that shit? I'ma tell you what son . . . Nah, I'ma go to school, I'ma be

President and I'ma blow niggas whole countries up all over the Earth and I'ma make bank! Understand *that* shit!

..You see that Lexus right there? That Lexus fat boy. I'ma own Lexus, Jeep . . . Oh Shit! I told you I'm gettin a Jeep? Word to god kid, Red, Cherokee, 91. I'ma have the bomb system in that shit too. Bensi, equalizer . . . Cause I had saved up bills from that jail job. Hey yo, seven hundred cells we gonna build in that shit. We gonna lock niggas heads up all day in that motherfucker right? So I'm sayin, already I got the Bensi, I got the equalizer. All I got to get is um, the Jeep, and the insurance. Yo you should give me your beeper number, we should hang out. ..You don't got a beeper? How somebody supposed to get in touch with you then? ..The phone? Daha. This nigga livin like Fred Flintstone yo.

On the reals though, I gotta pick up my little brother and get my food. I'ma call you then. ..It's good to see you though right? Right. Hey yo Al, they still givin out applications for that shit that you doin? I'm sayin though. Oh next year? Yeah I might peep that shit out, definitely though. Aight then. I'ma call you then. Right. One love god.

[*Flex takes a moment and re-enters the take-out.*] Hey yo son. Yo son! Oh you don't see me now? I said you don't see me right now. You aint tryin to serve me now? Nevermind son, my shit's ready? . . . How you know that's mine though? It's in a bag, I can't see that shit. That could be my man's right there. Aight then, I'ma tell you what, lemme get extra duck sauce, hot sauce, napkins, all that shit kid. You know extra? Lemme get extra . . . $3.25? $3.25. Don't be tryin to jerk me neither man. This nigga tryin to be slick, fuckin immigrant-ass motherfucker . . . I said

SOME PEOPLE

you a immigrant. You know what I'm sayin? You aint from here, I'm *from* here. Know that shit.

How I know what? How I know I'm from here? Nigga can't even talk English talkin bout how I know. What you know? You don't know shit! I'm American son. You aint shit! Gimme my shit yo. [*Flex takes his food and motions to leave but then turns back.*] . . . Hey yo boy, you don't say thank you? Yeah, you're welcome. Know your place yo. I know mine.

CÉSAR

[César is fifty-ish and is at his first visit to a psychotherapist. He wears a traditional guayabera and hat, and carries a cowbell and stick. He sings the first verse of Eddie Palmieri's "Te Palo Pa Rumba" and tries to accompany it with the cowbell.]

I don't play, I just hit it. Because is very difficult if you want to play that. Is not just that you hit it. You have to know what's the rhythm, the music, you have to be musician. Lotta people thinking is just that you hit it. No no. I don't sing also but that song, my favorite song. "Te Palo Pa Rumba." The guy who make that song is very famous guy. His name is Eddie Palmieri. That guy, hooh, famous. You ever listen to salsa music? He play piano, and also he tell all the musician what to play. So, if is the trombone, or the trumpet, or the drum or whatever. He gonna explain to them, he's a composer, he compose all the music there. He very famous that guy. ..So you tell me to bring something that I gonna remember what happen, so I bring that [*cowbell and stick*]. That, I buy to my son when he have only one year old. He never really play because he never listen to salsa music. He only wanna listen to the fast music I don't know how you call it.

. . . Also I bring that [*hat*]. That I buy to my son when he have ten, eleven years old. He put in the head and he go in the street and he pretend that he Cary Grant. You know Cary Grant? The famous guy? He put in the head for one week and then he throw in the shelf and he never wear. But I keep it because that's my son. So, I supposed to talk to you forty-five minutes, I don't know what you want me to say. No because my wife, she make me come here. Because in my place if you have a problem, you never talking to a therapist. Forget it. In my place if you go to a therapist, they say you crazy in the head. If my friends know I coming here, forget it. They gonna say, César go crazy. But I trust my wife. She's very modern, moderna, you know, modern. Very up to date. She reading all the magazine. She gonna look the magazine, then she gonna tell me what I has to do.

Because in my place, if you have a problem, you has to go and talking with un santero o una santera, is like, una consejera. Is a woman, or man, is depend. And she have power, and she take you hand, and she looking you hand, and she tell you what's you problem. Then she tell you you has to take some plant, some herbs, some spices. And you put in the pot. And then you put fire, or some flame there, and you make all the bad thing go out the whole place. Or maybe you put some water, is depend what's you problem.

..So, my son, he always have a good heart. He never say bad words to nobody, he never punching to nobody. I remember when he have maybe five, six years old. I'm walking to him, with him en the Prospect Park, allá en Brooklyn. And it's the bird. Some bird, the pigeon, is laying in the floor because it's some truck or something gonna come and hit the bird. So the bird laying there in the floor. So my son, he running the bird. He wanna fix it. He say to the bird, Hey bird, what's the matter with you? You has to get up from there. Is no good that you laying there. You has to go fly . . . up in there. But the bird is only looking in the sky, because the bird know in five minutes, it's no more. He wanna take the bird home. I say, you can't take it, the bird is dirty, is from the street. Quería poner como un Band-Aid. But he have a good heart . . . Maybe when he get a little older, he put some fancy clothes. Not fancy, pero whatever. He put some cologne . . . Lotta cologne my son putting there. He go with the girlfriend in the high school. Because he very handsome. He like me, very handsome. I told to my son, Be careful. Also I told him, César I love you. His name is César like my name is César. I make sure I gonna tell him to that.

Because I see in the TV en Oprah Winfrey, is some people. They have five kid, three kid, seven kid. Never say I love you. Only they put the hand, throwing out, and what's the kid? Drug, in the street, problems, whatever. Me and my wife, we only having one kid, César. I always making sure I gonna tell to him César I love you. ..He say to me all the time, Papi I know. Because he don't wanna hear. He wanna be man. But I telling that to him anyway.

..When he have one year old, I have a big party for him. I invite all the relative from my family, my wife family. They coming all the way from Puerto Rico. Also we have some people from Dominican Republic. New Jersey, Long Island, Connecticut. All coming to my house in New York City for my son gonna have one year old. Almost one hundred people in my house coming. My wife and her sister is cooking. If you ever taste what they cooking that day, you gonna be like, Oh my God, forget it. It's a lotta dancing in there. It's one place in the party I say to all the people, shut up you mouth. Because my son César gonna play "Te Palo Pa Rumba." That song that I told you before. Because that song is come in the Spanish radio station, en ese mismo tiempo when he have one year old. Maybe fifteen, sixteen years ago. Fifteen years.

So I putting him the lap. I put the bell the hand. Because is very heavy, he can't lift it he only have one year. I put the hand the stick. And everybody is looking. And we play "Te Palo Pa Rumba." The whole song. And it's a long song. And everybody is, wow! I never forget that moment there. Because it's very special to me, that time. That whole time, I taking that time, I put it in here [*He points to his heart.*] . . . Four months ago, he come to me, he say, Papi I'm going out. I say where you going? He say, to the movie. I say ok, be careful. I told him, César I love you. He say, Papi I know . . . That's when I lose him . . . Is very difficult because the police told is some accident that he's running, the police shooting to him but, whatever. No because, my wife she working and then she coming home always cry. And I working, and in the night, I never sleep. How I gonna work if I never sleep? She told me, you better go to sleep. I told her, well you better stop cry entónces. She told me, César if you feeling bad, you has to take all the people in the whole world that love you, and you putting those people here [*he points to his heart again*] and it's gonna making that you feeling warm in here.

So I thinking, who love me? My wife love me, put it here. My sister love me, put it here. My two brother love me . . . My César love me, put it here. And I know that he love me because that day when he go to the movie he say, Papi I love you too. It's the only time he say that, but I hear that. Pero very cold in here . . . I told my wife, you has to get some better magazine because that's no working. All the time I thinking that he's sitting there and play that, but whatever. I miss him. Maybe I should never coming here, maybe I go talking to some people because maybe you don't listening to me . . . [*César sings the first verse of "Te Palo Pa Rumba" as lights fade out.*]

ROUGHNECK CHICKEN (EPILOGUE)

[*Roughneck Chicken is a mythical character somewhere between Jamaican Dub Poet, Sage and Chicken. He wears Red, Gold and Green and sunglasses. He beats on the wooden cube to provide the music for this poem which is done in song.*]

I hope you don't mind if I keep you, just a few likkle minutes after

And if you don't feel like stayin, den get the hell outta de theater

But you clap at the end of my show, so I take it you were listenin

I hope you have enjoy youself, but listen to this one more thing

Ey . . .

I know that some of you people have never seen Brooklyn or Bronx

That's very funny to me. Ha ha ha ha ha ha ha.

But that's not really the subject of this last and final part

So let me collect my thoughts together correctly so that I can start . . .

And remember you came to see theatre, this aint no performance art.

Some People

I want to give you two words, so dat you can take dem with you

Now don't say dem loud goin home pon de train, because somebody might hit you

The first word is Dem. That means Dem, those people over there

The second word is We. That means Us, these people over here

Now I hear alotta people talkin, about DemDem, Those people and ting,

Dem Terrorist Muslim Crack Addict AIDS Baby Bad Guy Doin De Tiefin

Now when I hear people say We, they always feelin happy

Like We make Three Billion Dolla Spaceship, put inna sky, aint dat nifty?

We make Three Thousand Talk Shows, and the people love it

We Kill Three Billion Chickens this year, and make dem inna Chicken Nugget

We made Three Billion Dollars, but We gave money to the poor

We dropped big bombs on those evil fucked up people and We won the war

Ey . . .

Last month I talk to a Chicken, by the name of Bingi

So pay attention good now, I goin tell you what the Chicken tole me

Long long time ago . . . Chickens ran de Earth

About A Hundred Fifty Thousand Years, before People was birth

The Chickens used to live in big mansions, and the other birds live in the street

The Chickens used to drive BMW, and the other birds walk with dem feet

The Chickens used to say, Look at dem birds, dem filthy lazy bum

How can they live like that really, We are so smart and Dem so dumb

Well today all de Chickens die, and the other birds fly in the sky

That was the end of his story, ha ha ha ha ha ha ha

Ey . . .

Last verse, then you go home.

If you don't know my name, me a de Roughneck Chicken me run de area

And any dibby dibby DJ wan to come try tes me dem ago get murda

I want you to know I am the number one dancehall chicken inna New York City

And to all de young sexy lady, I want you to know I'm young single and free

So if you want my phone number, well you must come get it from me

Or take youself a visit to Brooklyn, and just ask fe de Dancehall Daddy.

Ey . . .

PHOTO CREDITS

Characters/photo credits (clockwise, from top left): Caribbean Tiger (Will Hart/Courtesy HBO); Al Capón (Paula Court); Doris (Paula Court); Floe (Paula Court); Kazmierczack (Dona Ann McAdams); Bill (Dona Ann McAdams); Roughneck Chicken (Will Hart/Courtesy HBO); Blanca (Paula Court). Center photo: César (Paula Court).

ABOUT THE AUTHOR

Danny Hoch is a third-generation New Yorker who received an OBIE award for *Some People* at Performance Space 122 and The Joseph Papp Public Theater in 1994, and was nominated for a 1995 Drama Desk Award. The television version of *Some People* can be seen on HBO, and was nominated for a 1996 Cable Ace Award. Mr. Hoch spent four years bringing conflict-resolution-through-drama to adolescents in New York City's jails and alternative high schools with NYU's Creative Arts Team. A graduate of New York City's High School of Performing Arts, he also trained at the North Carolina School Of The Arts and in London. Mr. Hoch has written and acted for television and several films including HBO's *Subway Stories* and Terrence Malick's *Thin Red Line*. His play *Clinic Con Class* appeared as part of *Pieces Of The Quilt*. He is the recipient of a Solo Theatre Fellowship from the National Endowment For The Arts, a 1996 Sundance Screenwriters Fellow, and was just named a 1998 recipient of a CalArts/Alpert Award In Theatre and a 1999 Tennessee Williams Playwrights Fellow. Mr. Hoch's writing has been published in *Harper's*, *The New Theater Review* and *Out Of Character*. His third show, *Jails, Hospitals & Hip-Hop*, premiered at Berkeley Reperatory Theater in 1997, and will open in New York City in March 1998.